THE
COCKATOUCAN

E. NESBIT

Illustrated by
Elroy Hughes

Beehive Books

Matilda's ears were red and shiny. So were her cheeks. Her hands were red too. This was because Pridmore had washed her. It was not the usual washing, which makes you clean and comfortable, but the 'thorough good wash', which makes you burn and smart.

"Other children," said Matilda, "don't have their ears washed thoroughly, and they don't have new dresses that are prickly in the insides round their arms, and cut them round the neck. Do they, Pridmore?"

But Pridmore only said, "Stuff and nonsense," and then she said, "don't wriggle so, child, for goodness' sake."

Pridmore was Matilda's nursemaid. Matilda sometimes found her trying. She was taking the over-washed, over-brushed, over-combed, gloved, booted, and hatted Matilda in an omnibus to Streatham to see her Great-aunt Willoughby. Her mother had arranged for it. Pridmore had prepared her for it. Matilda, knowing resistance to be in vain, had submitted to it.

But destiny had not been consulted, and destiny had plans of its own for Matilda.

When the last button of Matilda's boots had been fastened (the button hook always had a nasty temper, especially when it was hurried, and that day it bit a little piece of Matilda's leg quite spitefully) the wretched child was taken downstairs and put on a chair in the hall to wait while Pridmore popped her own things on.

"I shan't be a minute," said Pridmore. Matilda knew better. She seated herself to wait and swung her legs miserably. She had been to her Great-aunt Willoughby's before, and she knew exactly what to expect. She would be

2

asked about her lessons, and how many
marks she had, and whether she had been a
good girl. I can't think why grown-up people don't
see how impertinent these questions are. Suppose you were to answer, "I'm
top of my class, Auntie, thank you, and I'm very good. And now let's have
a little talk about you. Aunt, dear, how much money have you got, and have
you been scolding the servants again, or have you tried to be good and patient
as a properly brought-up aunt should be, eh, dear?"

Try this method with one of your aunts next time she begins asking you
questions, and write and tell me what she says.

3

Matilda knew exactly what the Aunt Willoughby's questions would be, and she knew how, when they were answered, her aunt would give her a small biscuit with caraway seeds in it, and then tell her to go with Pridmore and have her hands and face washed again.

Then she should be sent to walk in the garden — the garden had a gritty path, and geraniums and calceolarias and lobelias in the beds. You might not pick anything. There would be minced veal at dinner with three-cornered bits of toast round the dish, and a tapioca pudding. Then the long afternoon with a book, a bound volume with nasty small print, and all the stories about children who died young because they were too good for this world.

Matilda wriggled wretchedly. If she had been a little less uncomfortable she would have cried, but her new frock was too tight and prickly to let her forget it for a moment, even in tears.

When Pridmore came down at last, she said, "Fie, for shame! What a sulky face!"

And Matilda said, "I'm not."

"Oh, yes you are," said Pridmore, "you know you are, you don't appreciate your blessings."

"I wish it was your Aunt Willoughby," said Matilda.

"Nasty, spiteful little thing!" said Pridmore, and she shook Matilda.

Then Matilda tried to slap Pridmore, and the two went down the steps not at all pleased with each other. They went down the dull road to the dull omnibus, and Matilda was crying a little.

Now Pridmore was a very careful person, though cross, but even the most

4

careful persons make mistakes sometimes — and she must have taken the wrong omnibus, or this story could never have happened, and where would we all have been then? This shows you that even mistakes are sometimes valuable, so do not be hard on grown-ups if they are wrong sometimes. You know after all, it hardly ever happens.

It was a very bright green and gold omnibus, and inside the cushions were green and very soft. Matilda and her nursemaid had it all to themselves, and Matilda began to feel more comfortable, especially as she had wriggled till she had burst one of her shoulder seams and got more room for herself inside her frock.

So she said, "I'm sorry I was cross, Priddy dear."

Pridmore said, "So you ought to be." But she never said *she* was sorry for being cross. But you must not expect grown-up people to say that.

It was certainly the wrong omnibus because instead of jolting slowly along dusty streets, it went quickly and smoothly down a green lane, with flowers in the hedges, and green trees overhead. Matilda was so delighted that she sat quite still, a very rare thing with her. Pridmore was reading a penny story called *The Vengeance of the Lady Constantia*, so she did not notice anything.

"I don't care. I shan't tell her," said Matilda. "She'd stop the bus as likely as not."

At last the omnibus stopped of its own accord. Pridmore put her story in her pocket and began to get out.

"Well, I never!" she said, and got out very quickly and ran round to where the horses were. They were white horses with green harnesses, and their tails were very long indeed.

"Hi, young man!" said Pridmore to the omnibus driver. "You've brought us to the wrong place. This isn't Streatham Common, this isn't."

The driver was the most beautiful omnibus driver you ever saw, and his clothes were like him in beauty. He had white silk stockings and a ruffled silk shirt of white, and his coat and breeches were green and gold. So was his three-cornered hat which he lifted politely when Pridmore spoke to him.

"I fear," he said kindly, "that you must have taken, by some unfortunate misunderstanding, the wrong omnibus."

"When does the next go back?"

"The omnibus does not go back. It runs from Brixton here once a month, but it doesn't go back."

"But how does it get to Brixton again, to start again, I mean?" asked Matilda.

"We start a new one every time," said the driver, raising his three-cornered hat once more.

"And what becomes of the old ones?" Matilda asked.

"Ah," said the driver, smiling, "that depends. One never knows before hand, things change so nowadays. Good morning. Thank you so much for your patronage. No, on no account, Madam."

He waved away the eight pence which Pridmore was trying to offer him for the fare from Brixton, and drove quickly off.

When they looked around them, no, this was certainly not Streatham Common. The wrong omnibus had brought them to a strange village — the neatest, sweetest, reddest, greenest, cleanest, prettiest village in the world. The houses were grouped round in a village green, on which children in pretty loose frocks or smocks were playing happily.

Not a tight armhole was to be seen, or even imagined in that happy spot. Matilda swelled herself out and burst three hooks and a bit more of the shoulder seam.

The shops seemed a little queer, Matilda thought. The names somehow did not match the things that were to be sold. For instance, where it said 'Elias Groves, Tinsmith', there were loaves and buns in the window, and the shop that had 'Baker' over the door, was full of perambulators — the grocer and the wheelwright seemed to have changed names, or shops, or something — and Miss Skimpling, dressmaker or milliner, had her shop window full of pork and sausage meat.

"What a funny, nice place," said Matilda. "I am glad we took the wrong

omnibus.''

A little boy in a yellow smock had come up close to them.

''I beg your pardon,'' he said very politely, ''but all strangers are brought before the King at once. Please follow me.''

''Well, of all the impudence,'' said Pridmore. ''Strangers, indeed! And who may you be, I should like to know?''

''I,'' said the little boy, bowing very low, ''am the Prime Minister. I know I do not look it, but appearances are deceptive. It's only for a short time. I shall probably be myself again by tomorrow.''

Pridmore muttered something which the little boy did not hear. Matilda caught a few words. ''Smacked'', ''bed'', ''bread and water'' — familiar words all of them.

''If it's a game,'' said Matilda to the boy, ''I should like to play.''

He frowned.

''I advise you to come at once,'' he said, so sternly that even Pridmore was a little frightened. ''His Majesty's palace is in this direction.'' He walked away, and Matilda made a sudden jump, dragged her hand out of Pridmore's, and ran after him. So Pridmore had to follow, still grumbling.

The palace stood in a great green park dotted with white-flowered bushes. It was not at all like an English palace, St. James's or Buckingham Palace, for instance, because it was very beautiful and very clean. When they got in they saw that the palace was hung with green silk. The footmen had green and gold liveries, and all the courtiers' clothes were the same colours.

Matilda and Pridmore had to wait a few moments while the King changed his sceptre and put on a clean crown, and then they were shown into the audience chamber. The King came to meet them.

"It is kind of you to have come so far," he said. "Of course you'll stay at the palace?" He looked anxiously at Matilda.

"Are you *quite* comfortable, my dear?" he asked doubtfully.

Matilda was very truthful — for a girl.

"No," she said, "my frock cuts me round the arms —"

"Ah," he said, "and you brought no luggage — some of the Princess's frocks — her old ones perhaps? This person — your maid, no doubt?"

A loud laugh rang suddenly through the hall. The King looked uneasily round, as though he expected something to happen. But nothing seemed likely to occur.

"Yes," said Matilda, "Pridmore is — oh, dear!"

For before her eyes she saw an awful change taking place in Pridmore. In an instant all that was left of the original Pridmore were the boots and the hem of her skirt — the top part of her had changed into painted iron and glass, and even as Matilda looked the bit of skirt that was left got flat and hard and square. The two feet turned into four feet, and they were iron feet,

10

and there was no more Pridmore.

"Oh, my poor child," said the King, "your maid has turned into an automatic machine."

It was too true. The maid had turned into a machine such as those which you see in a railway station — greedy, grasping things which take your pennies and give you next to nothing in chocolate and no change.

But there was no chocolate to be seen through the glass of the machine that once had been Pridmore. Only little rolls of paper.

The King silently handed some pennies to Matilda. She dropped one into the machine and pulled out the little drawer. There was a scroll of paper. Matilda opened it and read: "Don't be tiresome."

She tried again. This time it was: "If you don't give over I'll tell your ma first thing when she comes home."

The next was: "Go along with you do — always worrying"; so then Matilda *knew*.

"Yes," said the King sadly. "I fear there's no doubt about it. Your maid has turned into an automatic nagging machine. Never mind, my dear, she'll be all right tomorrow."

"I like her best like this, thank you," said Matilda quickly. "I needn't put in any more pennies, you see."

"Oh, we mustn't be unkind and neglectful," said the King gently, and he dropped in a penny. He got:

"You tiresome boy, you. Leave me be this minute."

"I can't help it," said the King wearily; "you've no idea how suddenly things change here. It's because — but I'll tell you all about it at tea time. It is a long story to tell. Go with nurse now, my dear, and see if any of the Princess's frocks will fit you."

Then a nice, kind, cuddly nurse led Matilda away to the Princess's apartments, and took off the stiff frock that hurt, and put on a green silk gown, as soft as birds' breasts, and Matilda kissed her for the sheer joy at being so comfortable.

"And now, dearie," said the nurse, "you'd like to see the Princess, wouldn't you? Take care you don't hurt yourself with her. She's rather sharp."

Matilda did not understand this then. Afterwards she did.

The nurse took her through many marble corridors and up and down many marble steps, and at last they came to a garden full of white roses, and in the middle of it, on a green satin-covered eiderdown, as big as a feather bed, sat the Princess in a white gown.

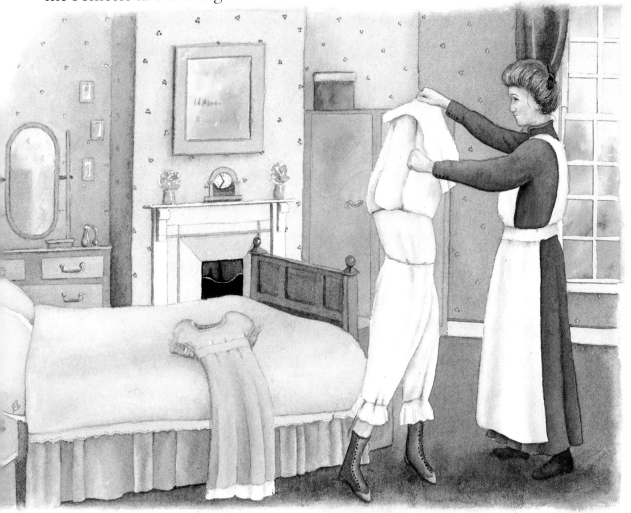

She got up when Matilda came towards her, and it was like seeing a yard and a half of white tape stand up on one end and bow — a yard and a half of broad white tape, of course; but what is considered to be broad for tape is very narrow indeed for princesses.

"How are you?" said Matilda, who had been taught manners.

"Very slim indeed, thank you," said the Princess. And she was. Her face was so white and thin that it looked as though it were made of an oyster shell. Her hands were thin and white, and her fingers reminded Matilda of fish bones. Her hair and eyes were black and Matilda thought she might have been pretty if she had been fatter. When she shook hands with Matilda her bony fingers hurt quite hard.

The Princess seemed pleased to see her visitor, and invited her to sit with Her Highness on the satin cushion.

"I have to be very careful or I should break," said she; "that's why the cushion is so soft, and I can't play many games for fear of accidents. Do you know any sitting-down games?"

The only thing Matilda could think of was cat's cradle, so they played that with the Princess's green hair-ribbon. Her fish-bony fingers were much cleverer than Matilda's little fat, pink paws.

Matilda looked about her between the games and admired everthing very much, and asked questions, of course. There was a very large bird chained to a perch in the middle of a very large cage. Indeed the cage was so big that it took up all one side of the rose garden. The bird had a yellow crest like a cockatoo and a very large bill like a toucan. (If you do not know what a toucan is you do not deserve ever to go to the zoological gardens again.)

"What is that bird?" asked Matilda.

14

"Oh," said the Princess, "that's my pet Cockatoucan; he's very valuable.
If he were to die or be stolen the Green Land would wither up and grow like
New Cross or Islington."

"How horrible!" said Matilda.

"I've never been to those places, of
course," said the Princess, shuddering,
"but I hope I know my geography."

"All of it?" asked Matilda.

15

"Even the exports and imports," said the Princess. "Good-bye, I'm so thin I have to rest a good deal or I should wear myself out. Nurse, take her away."

So the nurse took her away to a wonderful room, where she amused herself till tea time with all the kind of toys that you see and want in the shop when someone is buying you a box of bricks or a puzzle map — the kind of toys you never get because they are so expensive.

Matilda had tea with the King. He was full of true politeness and treated Matilda exactly as though she had been a grown-up — so that she was extremely happy and behaved beautifully. The King told her all his troubles.

"You see," he began, "what a pretty place my Green Land was once. It has points even now. But things aren't what they used to be. It's that bird, that Cockatoucan. We daren't kill it or give it away. And every time it laughs something changes. Look at my Prime Minister. He was a six-foot man. And look at him now. I could lift him with one hand. And then your poor maid. It's all that bad bird."

"Why *does* it laugh?" asked Matilda.

"I can't think," said the King. "I can't see anything to laugh at."

"Can't you give it lessons, or something nasty to make it miserable?"

"I have, I do, I assure you, my dear child. The lessons that bird has to swallow would choke a professor."

"Does it eat anything else besides lessons?"

"Christmas Pudding. But there — what's the use of talking — that bird would laugh if it were fed on dog biscuits."

His Majesty sighed and passed the buttered toast.

"You can't possibly," he went on, "have any idea of the kind of things that happen. That bird laughed one day at a cabinet council, and all my ministers turned into little boys in yellow smocks; and we can't get any laws made till they come right again. It's not their fault, and I must keep their situations open for them, of course, poor things."

"Of course," said Matilda.

"There was a dragon, now," said the King. "When he came I offered the Princess's hand and half my kingdom to any one who would kill him. It's an offer that is always made, you know."

17

"Yes," said Matilda.

"Well, a respectable young Prince came along, and every one turned out to see him fight the dragon. As much as ninepence each was paid for the front seats, I assure you. The trumpet sounded and the dragon came hurrying up. A trumpet is like a dinner-bell to a dragon, you know. And the Prince drew his bright sword and we all shouted, and then that wretched bird laughed and the dragon turned into a pussycat, and the Prince killed it before he could stop himself. The populace was furious."

"What happened then?" asked Matilda.

"Well, I did what I could. I said, 'You shall marry the Princess just the same.' So I brought the Prince home, and when we got there the Cockatoucan had just been laughing again, and the Princess had turned into a very old German governess. The Prince went home in a great hurry and an awful temper. The Princess was all right in a day or two. These are trying times, my dear."

"I am so sorry for you," said Matilda, going on with the preserved ginger.

"Well you may be," said the miserable Monarch, "but if I were to try to tell you all that that bird has brought on my poor kingdom I should keep you up till long past your proper bedtime."

"I don't mind," said Matilda kindly. "Do tell me some more."

"Why," the King went on, growing now more agitated, "why, at one titter from that revolting bird the long row of ancestors on my palace wall grew red-faced and vulgar; they began to drop their haitches and to assert that their name was Smith from Clapham Junction."

18

"How dreadful!"

"And once," said the King in a whimper, "it laughed so loudly that two Sundays came together and next Thursday got lost, and went prowling away and hid itself on the other side of Christmas. And now," he said suddenly, "it's bedtime."

"Must I go?" asked Matilda.

"Yes please," said the King. "I tell all strangers this tragic story because I always feel that perhaps some stranger might be clever enough to help me. You seem a very nice little girl. Do you think you are clever?"

It is very nice even to be asked if you are clever. Your Aunt Willoughby knows well enough that you are not. But kings do say nice things. Matilda was very pleased.

19

"I don't think I am clever," she was saying quite honestly, when suddenly the sound of a hoarse laugh rang through the banqueting hall. Matilda put her hands to her head.

"Oh, dear!" she cried, "I feel so different. Oh! Wait a minute. Oh! Whatever is it? Oh!"

Then she was silent for a moment. Then she looked at the King and said, "I was wrong, Your Majesty, I *am* clever, and I know it is not good for me to sit up late. Good night. Thank you so much for your nice party. In the morning I think I shall be clever enough to help you, unless the bird laughs me back into the other kind of Matilda."

But in the morning Matilda's head felt strangely clear; only when she came down to breakfast full of plans for helping the King, she found that the Cockatoucan must have laughed in the night, for the beautiful palace had turned into a butcher's shop, and the King, who was too wise to fight against fate, had tucked up his royal robes, and was busy in the shop weighing out six ounces of the best mutton chops for a child with a basket.

"I don't know how even you can help me now," he said despairingly; "as long as the palace stays like this, it's no use trying to go on with being a king, or anything. I can only try to be a good butcher. You shall keep the accounts if you like, till that bird laughs me back into my palace again."

So the King settled down to business, respected by his subjects, who had all, since the coming of the Cockatoucan, had their little ups and downs. And Matilda kept the books and wrote out the bills, and really they were both rather happy. Pridmore, disguised as the automatic machine, stood in the shop and attracted many customers. They used to bring their children,

and make the poor innocents put their pennies in, and then read Pridmore's good advice. Some parents are so harsh. And the Princess sat in the back garden with the Cockatoucan, and Matilda played with her every afternoon. But one day, as the King was driving through another kingdom, the King of that kingdom looked out of one of his palace windows, and laughed as the King went by, and shouted, "Butcher!"

The butcher-king did not mind this, because it was true, however rude. But when the other King called out, "What price cat's meat?" the King was very angry indeed, because the meat he sold was always of the best quality. When he told Matilda all about it, she said, "Send an army to crush him."

So the King sent his army, and the enemy were crushed. The bird laughed the King back on to his throne and laughed away the butcher's shop just in time for His Majesty to proclaim a general holiday, and to organize a magnificent reception for the army. Matilda now helped the King to manage everything. She wonderfully enjoyed the delightful feeling of being clever, so that she felt it was indeed too bad when the Cockatoucan laughed just as the reception was beautifully arranged. It laughed, and the general holiday was turned into an income tax; the magnificent reception changed itself to a royal reprimand, and the army itself suddenly became a discontented Sunday-school treat, and had to be fed with buns and brought home in brakes, crying.

"Something must be done," said the King.

"Well," said Matilda, "I've been thinking if you will make me the Princess's governess, I'll see what I can do. I'm quite clever enough."

"I must open parliament to do that," said the King; "it's a constitutional change."

So he hurried off down the road to open parliament. But the bird put its head on one side and laughed at him as he went by. He hurried on, but his beautiful crown grew large and brassy, and was set with cheap glass

22

in the worst possible taste. His robe turned from velvet and ermine to flannelette and rabbit's fur. His sceptre grew twenty-feet long and extremely awkward to carry. But he persevered, his royal blood was up.

"No bird," he said, "shall keep me from my duty and my parliament."

But when he got there, he was so agitated that he could not remember which was the right key to open parliament with, and in the end he hampered the lock and so could not open parliament at all, and members of parliament went about making speeches in the roads to the great hindrance of the traffic.

The poor King went home and burst into tears.

"Matilda," he said, "this is too much. You have always been a comfort to me. You stood by me when I was a butcher; you kept the books; you booked the orders; you ordered the stock. If you really are clever enough, now is the time to help me. If you won't, I'll give up the business. I'll leave off being a king. I'll go and be a butcher in the Camberwell New Road, and I will get another little girl to keep my books, not you."

This decided Matilda. She said, "Very well, Your Majesty, then give me leave to prowl at night. Perhaps I shall find out what makes the Cockatoucan laugh; if I can do that, we can take care he never gets it, whatever it is."

"Ah!" said the poor King, "If you could only do that."

When Matilda went to bed that night, she did not go to sleep. She lay and waited till all the palace was quiet, and then she crept softly, pussily, mousily to the garden, where the Cockatoucan's cage was, and she hid behind a white rosebush, and looked and listened. Nothing happened till it was grey dawn, and then it was only the Cockatoucan who woke up. But when the sun was round and red over the palace roof, something came creeping, creeping, pussily, mousily, out of the palace; and it looked like a yard and a half of white tape creeping along; and it was the Princess herself.

She came quietly up to the cage, and squeezed herself between the bars; they were very narrow bars, but a yard and a half of white tape can go through the bars of any bird cage I ever saw. And the Princess went up to the Cockatoucan and tickled him under his wings till he laughed aloud. Then, quick as thought, the Princess squeezed through the bars, and was back in her room before the bird had finished laughing. Matilda went back to bed.

Next day all the sparrows had turned into cart horses, and the roads were impassable.

That day when she went, as usual, to play with the Princess, Matilda said to her suddenly, "Princess, what makes you so thin?"

The Princess caught Matilda's hand and pressed it with warmth.

"Matilda," she said simply, "you have a noble heart. No one else has ever asked me that, though they tried to cure it. And I couldn't answer till I was asked, could I? It's a sad, a tragic tale, Matilda. I was once as fat as you are."

"I'm not so very fat," said Matilda, indignantly.

"Well," said the Princess, impatiently, "I was quite fat enough anyhow. And then I got thin —"

"But how?"

"Because they would not let me have my favourite pudding every day."

"What a shame!" said Matilda. "And what is your favourite pudding?"

Bread and milk, of course, sprinkled with rose leaves — and with pear-drops in it."

Of course, Matilda went at once to the King, and while she was on her way the Cockatoucan happened to laugh. When she reached the King, he was in no condition for ordering dinner, for he had turned into a villa-residence, replete with every modern improvement. Matilda only recognized him, as he stood sadly in the park, by the crown that stuck crookedly on one of the chimney pots, and the border of ermine along the garden path. So she ordered the Princess's favourite pudding on her own responsibility, and the whole court had it every day for dinner, till there was no single courtier but loathed the very sight of bread and milk, and there was hardly one who would not have run a mile than meet a pear-drop. Even Matilda herself got rather tired of it, though being clever, she knew how good bread and milk was for her.

But the Princess got fatter and fatter, and rosier and rosier. Her thread-paper gowns had to be let out, and then she had to wear the old ones that Matilda had been wearing, and then to have new ones. And as she got fatter she got kinder till Matilda grew quite fond of her.

And the Cockatoucan had not laughed for a month.

When the Princess was as fat as any Princess ought to be, Matilda went to her one day, and threw her arms round her and kissed her. The Princess kissed her back, and said, "Very well, I *am* sorry then, but I didn't want to say so, but now I will. And the Cockatoucan never laughs except when he's tickled. So there! He hates to laugh."

"And you won't do it again," said Matilda, "will you?"

"No, of course not," said the Princess, very much surprised, "why should I? I was spiteful when I was thin, but now I'm fat again I want every one to be happy."

"But how can any one be happy," asked Matilda severely, "when every one is turned into something they weren't meant to be? There's your dear father — he's a desirable villa — the Prime Minister was a little boy, and he got back again, and now he's turned into a comic opera. Half the palace housemaids are breakers, dashing themselves against the palace crockery: the navy to a man, are changed to French poodles, and the army to German sausages. Your favourite nurse is now a flourishing steam laundry, and I, alas, am too clever by half. Can't that horrible bird do anything to put us all right again?"

"No," said the Princess, dissolving in tears at this awful picture, "he told me once himself that when he laughed he could only change one or two things at once, and then, as often as not, it turned out to be something he didn't expect. The only way to make everything come right again would be — but it can't be done! If we could only make him laugh on the wrong side of his face. That's the secret. He told me so. But I don't know what it *is*, let alone being able to do it. Could *you* do it, Matilda?"

"No," said Matilda, "but let me whisper. He's listening. Pridmore could. She's often told me she'd do it to me. But she never has. Oh, Princess, I've got an idea."

The two were whispering so low that the Cockatoucan could not hear, though he tried his hardest. Matilda and the Princess left him listening.

Presently he heard the sound of wheels. Four men came into the rose-garden wheeling a great red thing in a barrow. They set it down in front of the Cockatoucan, who danced on his perch with rage.

"Oh," he said, "if only someone would make me laugh, that horrible thing would be the one to change. I know it would. It would change into something much horrider than it is now. I feel it in all my feathers."

The Princess opened the cage-door with the Prime Minister's key, which a tenor singer had found at the beginning of his music. It was also the key of the comic opera. She crept up behind the Cockatoucan and tickled him under both wings. He fixed his baleful eye on the red automatic machine and laughed long and loud; he saw the red iron and glass change before his eyes into the form of Pridmore. Her cheeks were red with rage and her eyes shone like glass with fury.

"Nice manners!" said she to the Cockatoucan. "What are you laughing at. I should like to know — I'll make you laugh on the wrong side of your face, my fine fellow!"

She sprang into the cage, and then and there, before the astonished court, she shook that Cockatoucan till he really and truly did laugh on the wrong side of his face. It was a terrible sight to witness, and the sound of that wrong-sided laughter was horrible to hear.

But instantly all the things changed back as if by magic to what they had been before. The laundry became a nurse, the villa became a king, the other people were just what they had been before, and all Matilda's wonderful cleverness went out like the snuff of a candle.

The Cockatoucan himself fell in two — one half of him became a common, ordinary toucan, such as you must have seen a hundred times at the zoo,

unless you are unworthy to visit that happy place, and the other half became a
weathercock, which, as you know, is always changing and makes the wind
change too. So he has not quite lost his old power. Only now he is in halves,
any power he may have has to be used without laughing. The poor, broken
Cockatoucan, like King you-know-who in English history, has never since
that sad day smiled again.

The grateful King sent an escort of the whole army, now no longer dressed in sausage skins, but in uniforms of dazzling beauty, with drums and banners, to see Matilda and Pridmore home. But Matilda was very sleepy. She had been clever for so long that she was quite tired out. It is indeed a very fatiguing thing, as no doubt you know. And the soldiers must have been sleepy too, for one by one the whole army disappeared, and by the time Pridmore and Matilda reached home there was only one left, and he was the policeman at the corner.

The next day Matilda began to talk to Pridmore about the Green Land and the Cockatoucan and the Villa-Residence-King, but Pridmore only said:

"Pack of nonsense! Hold your tongue, do!"

So Matilda naturally understood that Pridmore did not wish to be reminded of the time when she was an automatic nagging machine, so of course, like a kind and polite little girl, she let the subject drop.

Matilda did not mention her adventures to the others at home because she knew they believed her to have spent the time with her Great-aunt Willoughby. And she knew if she had said that she had not been there she would be sent at once — and she did not wish this.

She has often tried to get Pridmore to take the wrong omnibus again, which is the only way she knows of getting to the Green Land; but only once has she been successful, and

then the omnibus did not go to the Green Land at all, but to the Elephant and Castle.

But no little girl ought to expect to go to the Green Land more than once in a lifetime. Many of us indeed are not even so fortunate as to go there once.

First published in 1901

This edition first published in Great Britain 1987 by
Beehive Books, an imprint of Macdonald & Company (Publishers) Limited,
Greater London House, Hampstead Road, London, NW1 7QX

A BPCC plc company

Typeset by Angel Graphics, London. Origination by Scancraft, London.
Printed in Spain by Novograph, S.A., Madrid

British Library Cataloguing in Publication Data

Nesbit, E.
The cockatoucan. —— (Nesbit picture book classics; 2).
I. Title II. Hughes, Elroy III. Series
823'.8 [J] PZ7

ISBN 0-356-13390-7